Three's Company, Mallory!

For my nieces and nephew,
Tillie, Hannah, Mimi, and Louis.
Love you all!
—Aunt Laurie

For my sweet little Juliette, who comforts me on
the sad days, cheers for me on the good days, and
gives me hope when I need it most.
—J.K.

Three's Company, Mallory!

by Laurie Friedman

illustrations by Jennifer Kalis

darby creek

MINNEAPOLIS

CONTENTS

 A Word from Mallory 6

Seeing Double 8

The New Girl 15

Dinner Disaster 31

A Switch-Up 43

Here, There, Everywhere 55

Operation *Three's a Crowd* 68

The Sleepover 83

Scissor (un)happy 99

All Alone 109

Planning Time 118

Wake-ups and Makeups 125

A Surprise! 145

Poetically Speaking 153

DIY Breakfast 156

A WORD FROM MALLORY

I, Mallory McDonald, officially love Saturday mornings. I love sleeping late. I love eating doughnuts. And I love watching my favorite TV show, *Fashion Fran*—especially because I always watch it with my best friend, Mary Ann.

That's what Mary Ann and I do on Saturday mornings. But this Saturday morning is different from other Saturday mornings.

It didn't start out different. I woke up. I brushed my teeth. I made my bed. I fed my cat, Cheeseburger, and then I fed myself. I was just finishing my doughnut and about to turn on the TV when I happened to look out the living room window.

That's when this Saturday morning started to be different from all other Saturday mornings.

I saw a moving truck parked in front of the house across the street. And I saw a girl who looked about my age standing in the front yard.

The girl looked just like Mary Ann. She was the same height as Mary Ann. She had the same blonde, curly hair as Mary Ann. She wore the same kind of jeans as Mary Ann and had on a shirt that looked just like one of Mary Ann's shirts. At first, I thought it was Mary Ann.

Then I saw something I hadn't expected. I saw Mary Ann!

She was crossing the street and walking toward the girl who looked just like her. She waved, and the other girl waved back. Then they started talking.

I rubbed my eyes to make sure I was seeing right. It was like Mary Ann had a long-lost twin I never knew about.

Seeing her left me with one big question: WHO IS THIS GIRL?

SEEING DOUBLE

"MOM!" I scream at the top of my lungs.

Mom is in the living room faster than Max can grab the TV remote out of my hand. "Mallory, are you OK?" she asks.

I hold Cheeseburger under one arm and point at the window with the other. "What's going on?" I ask.

Mom looks out the window and smiles like she actually likes what she sees. "The Fitzgeralds moved out, remember? It looks like the new family is moving in."

The Fitzgeralds moving out isn't what I'm talking about. Either Mom needs to get her glasses checked or she doesn't see what I see. I take a deep breath and try to calm myself down.

I ask Mom to look out the window again.

When she does, I start questioning her like I'm a lawyer and she's on the witness stand.

"Do you see a girl you've never seen before standing next to the moving truck?"

A DAY in COURT.

Just answer the question. | I swear to tell the truth.

Mom nods. "I do."

"Do you see my lifelong best friend, Mary Ann, talking to that girl?"

She nods again "Yes, I do."

"Did you notice that the girl you've never seen before looks a lot like Mary Ann?"

Mom puts her face closer to the glass. "My goodness. They do look very much alike." Her smile gets wider.

Right answer. Wrong reaction. Obviously Mom doesn't realize how weird it is that a girl who looks like my best friend is moving onto Wish Pond Road.

I make Mom sit down in one of the chairs by the window. Then I put Cheeseburger down and sit in the chair across from her. "Mom, why didn't you tell me that the people who are moving in have a daughter who looks like my best friend?"

Mom gives me a look like what I'm saying doesn't make much sense. "Mallory, I don't know anything about this family. I had no idea they have a daughter. And I certainly had no idea what she would look like. But isn't it nice that there's another girl on the street for you and Mary Ann to spend time with?"

I don't think Mom gets that I'm supposed to be the one asking the questions.

I look out the window again. Mary Ann and the new girl are still talking. The new girl is laughing. And so is Mary Ann! Mary Ann links her arm through the new girl's arm, and they walk toward her house. Together! I watch as they disappear through the front door.

The doughnut I ate for breakfast feels like it's doing backflips in my stomach.

I still don't really have an answer to my big question: WHO IS THIS GIRL?

For all I know, she could be an alien from outer space, sent here to carry out an evil plot . . . and what if she isn't the only alien? What if there are more of them coming?

I can see a whole army of aliens who look like everyone on Wish Pond Road. Joey. Max. Mom. Dad. Me! There might even be alien pets that look like Champ and Cheeseburger. I need to stop this invasion before it starts!

I face Mom and put my hands on her knees so she'll know that what I'm about to say is very important and she needs to listen to every word. "We need to find out more about these new neighbors."

"I agree," Mom says.

I breathe a sigh of relief. At least Mom understands the importance of this situation. Now we just have to figure out a plan.

But before I can start thinking about how to put Operation *Find Out What the Aliens Across the Street Are Doing Here* into action, Mom stands up and puts her sweater on.

She heads for the front door. I run in front of her to block the way.

"Mom, what are you doing?"

"I'm going to meet the new neighbors," she says like she's surprised I have to ask. Then she takes me by the arm and says three words I did NOT want to hear.

"You're coming too."

THE NEW GIRL

I follow Mom across the street, even though I'd like to turn back.

Mary Ann and the new girl are still inside the new girl's house, but now there's a lady standing in the front yard, watching the movers unload furniture.

When she sees Mom and me walking over, she smiles and waves like she's really happy to see us, even though she doesn't know who we are. She has long blonde hair

and big blue eyes and the whitest teeth
I've ever seen. I have to admit, she looks
more like a beauty pageant winner than
an alien.

"Welcome!" Mom says as we get close.
She introduces herself and then me.

"I'm Kate Jackson-Brown," says the
lady. She gives both of us big hugs. "It's
so nice of you to come say hello. This is
such a friendly neighborhood. My daughter
already made a friend, and we just got
here!"

*That new friend your daughter made is my
best friend.*

That's what I think, but I don't say it out
loud. Another thing I don't say out loud is
that it's weird to hug people you just met,
even if they are your neighbors.

If you ask me, this mom is a little too
sweet, like the time Mary Ann and I made

chocolate chip cookies and accidentally put the sugar in twice.

Mrs. Jackson-Brown says that she and her husband and daughter just moved to Fern Falls from Atlanta and that they don't know anyone here.

Mom starts telling Mrs. Jackson-Brown lots of stuff about Fern Falls.

I try to listen, but it's hard to act interested when my best friend is inside with some new girl and I'm stuck out here listening to a bunch of boring details about the grocery store, the dry cleaners and the pharmacy.

I glance at the door of the Jackson-Browns' house to see if Mary Ann and the new girl are coming back outside, but the only people coming in and out of the house are movers.

I think about my alien theory.

The truth is, Mrs. Jackson-Brown doesn't look like an alien or sound like an alien. Even though part of me would like to believe she and her daughter could get back in their spaceship and leave Wish Pond Road any minute, I know that's not the case.

When Mom finishes telling Mrs. Jackson-Brown all about Fern Falls, Mrs. Jackson-Brown switches her attention to me. "Mallory, what grade are you in?" she asks.

I hear myself telling her that I'm in fourth grade.

"Really? That's wonderful!" says Mrs. Jackson-Brown. "My daughter, Chloe Jennifer, is in fourth grade too."

Her daughter's name is Chloe Jennifer? Why doesn't she just go by Chloe or Jennifer? Nobody calls me Mallory Louise except Mom, and only when she's really mad at me.

"Is she finishing the school year at Fern Falls Elementary?" asks Mom.

"Yes," says Mrs. Jackson-Brown. "She starts on Monday morning. Her teacher is Mr. Knight."

"Wonderful!" says Mom. "Chloe Jennifer is in Mallory's class."

"That is wonderful!" says Mrs. Jackson-Brown.

It looks like I'm the only one who isn't sure if this is "wonderful." I haven't even met the new girl yet, and our moms are already acting like we're going to be friends, just because we live on the same street and are in the same class.

Before I have a chance to say anything, Chloe Jennifer and Mary Ann walk outside. No. Scratch that. They skip outside. Holding hands!

Mary Ann is holding hands and skipping

with a girl she hardly knows. Mary Ann and I haven't held hands while we skipped since we were in kindergarten!

"Mallory, you have to meet Chloe Jennifer," says Mary Ann as they skip over to where we're standing.

Chloe Jennifer smiles at me and says hi. Then Mary Ann starts talking like she's one big mouth that can't stop.

Way too much comes out of this!

Mary Ann's Mouth

"Chloe Jennifer's going to be in our class and her birthday is coming up and she said we can help her plan her party! You have to see her room. She has a purple rug and pink furniture! Her mom had the movers put her stuff on the moving truck last so they could take it off first, and now it's already all set up. It looks like she's been here forever. And check this out." Mary Ann puts her face up right next to Chloe Jennifer's. "Isn't it crazy how much we look alike? The movers could hardly tell us apart and Chloe Jennifer's dad took a picture of us and he said we look like sisters. And guess what else? Chloe Jennifer is a dancer, just like me! We're going to take hip-hop together. And we both have two names. Mary Ann and Chloe Jennifer. Get it? Chloe Jennifer said lots of girls at her old school in Atlanta had two names, but

I told her we're the only ones at Fern Falls Elementary with two names. Cool, huh?!?"

Cool isn't the word I would use. But for now I don't have to use any words at all, because Mary Ann is still talking.

"I asked Chloe Jennifer if she likes *Fashion Fran*. But she hadn't even heard of *Fashion Fran*. So I told her it's our favorite show and that we love to have sleepovers and watch *Fashion Fran* and paint our toenails, and now that she lives on Wish Pond Road, the three of us can do that stuff together! It's going to be. . ."

Mary Ann pauses—finally!—and looks at Chloe Jennifer.

"Fun, fun, fun!" they say at the same time. Then they both burst out laughing.

"I already told Chloe Jennifer how we like to say things three times," says Mary Ann.

I try to say something, but it's like

someone glued my mouth shut and nothing can come out.

When I woke up this morning, my life was completely normal. Now, a new girl who looks like my best friend has moved to my street, and my best friend thinks everything about her is cool. She's even invited her to do all the things the two of us have always done.

I don't know this girl yet. She might be nice. But if you ask me, best friends are supposed to do things together, not together with another person!

"Hey, Mallory, while the movers are at Chloe Jennifer's house, why don't we show her around the neighborhood?" Mary Ann says to me.

I try to give Mary Ann a *we're-supposed-to-be-watching*-Fashion-Fran-*not-showing-some-new-girl-around-the-neighborhood* look.

But Mary Ann doesn't notice. She's too busy telling Chloe Jennifer about the wish pond.

Mom and Mrs. Jackson-Brown are still talking about how nice it is that the three of us are all the same age and how funny it is that Mary Ann and Chloe Jennifer look so much alike.

"We'd love your family to come over for dinner tonight," I hear Mom saying to Mrs. Jackson-Brown.

I'm not sure why Mom thinks "we" would love this. The last time I checked, "we" meant more than one person.

I try to send a message from my brain to Mom's brain telling her to take back her invitation.

But my message-sending skills must be at an all-time low. Mom doesn't take back anything.

"That's so sweet of you. We'd love to come," says Mrs. Jackson-Brown.

Chloe Jennifer looks at me and smiles.

I try to smile back like I'm happy they're coming. But the truth is that I'm not so happy. In fact, if I had a piece of paper, I'd write down all the things I'm *not* happy about.

10 THINGS I, Mallory McDonald, AM NOT HAPPY ABOUT!

Thing #1: A new girl who looks just like my best friend moved to my street.

Thing #2: The new girl is a dancer, just like my best friend.

Thing #3: The new girl has two names, just like my best friend.

Thing #4: My best friend invited the new girl to do all our favorite things with us.

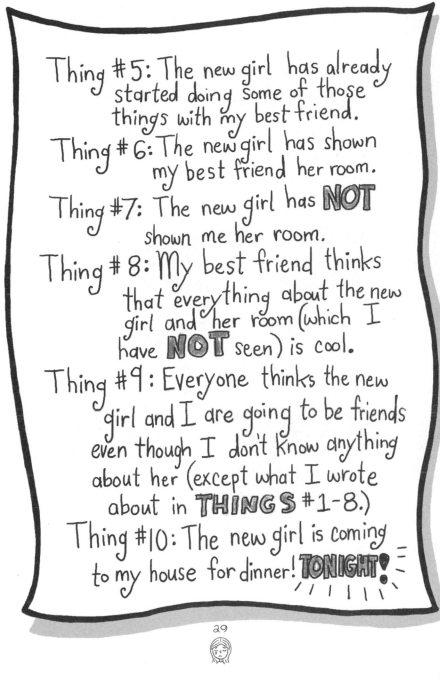

Thing #5: The new girl has already started doing some of those things with my best friend.

Thing #6: The new girl has shown my best friend her room.

Thing #7: The new girl has **NOT** shown me her room.

Thing #8: My best friend thinks that everything about the new girl and her room (which I have **NOT** seen) is cool.

Thing #9: Everyone thinks the new girl and I are going to be friends even though I don't know anything about her (except what I wrote about in **THINGS** #1-8.)

Thing #10: The new girl is coming to my house for dinner! **TONIGHT!**

While I'm thinking about all the things I'm not happy about, I hear Mom say something about inviting the Winstons to dinner too.

Mary Ann starts jumping up and down like this is as exciting as getting to meet Fashion Fran.

I look down the street toward the wish pond. I pretend I'm standing in front of it and make a wish.

I wish Chloe Jennifer Jackson-Brown would go back to where she came from.

But I know the only place Chloe Jennifer Jackson-Brown is going is to my house for dinner.

Tonight!

DINNER DISASTER

"Mallory, can you please set the table?" Mom hands me a stack of our good plates.

I feel like I'm carrying an armload of bowling balls. Our good plates are a lot heavier than our normal plates, and I have to be extra careful not to drop them. We only use them for special occasions. I don't see why tonight is a special occasion.

I head for the dining room. But it doesn't

seem fair that I have to set the table with our good plates when I didn't want to have this dinner in the first place.

When I finish, I decide to change clothes before dinner. I go to my room and look through my closet. I try to focus on what I'm going to wear, but all I can think about is Chloe Jennifer and Mary Ann holding hands and skipping. There's a picture of it in my brain, and it won't go away.

I wonder if Chloe Jennifer thinks she and Mary Ann are going to be best friends. I hope Mary Ann told her that *we're* best friends. But something tells me she didn't.

I pull on my purple skirt. "What top should I wear?" I ask Cheeseburger. I look at my cat, but she's asleep on my bed. She's not much help.

I open my T-shirt drawer and pull out the T-shirt on top. It's my pink *BFF* T-shirt.

Mary Ann has the same one. We bought them together at the mall.

Suddenly, I have a great idea!

I race back to the kitchen and pick up the phone. I dial the Winstons' number. Joey answers, and I ask him to get Mary Ann. When she finally picks up, I tell her to wear her *BFF* T-shirt tonight with her purple skirt.

She says she will.

Just hearing Mary Ann's voice makes me feel better.

"Tonight might not be so bad," I say to Cheeseburger when I get back to my room.

I slip on the T-shirt and look at myself in the mirror.

Part of me feels like maybe Mary Ann and I shouldn't dress alike tonight. Chloe Jennifer just moved here, and I don't want her to feel left out. But I also want her to know that Mary Ann and I are best friends and have been forever. Plus, Mary Ann and I always dress alike, so why should tonight be any different?

When the doorbell rings, Mom yells to everyone to come to the living room. I open the door for the Winstons—Frank, Colleen, Grandpa Winston, Winnie, Joey, and Mary Ann. As they walk inside, I smile and say hello to everyone.

But I stop smiling when I see Mary Ann. She's wearing her purple skirt. But she's NOT wearing her *BFF* T-shirt. She's wearing her *Fashion Rocks* T-shirt.

This night just went from *might-not-be-so-bad* to *BAD*. Whenever Mary Ann and I say

we're going to dress alike, we do. I cross my arms across my chest. "I thought you were going to wear your *BFF* shirt," I say to Mary Ann.

She shrugs. "I couldn't find it."

I start to say, "How could you lose your *BFF* T-shirt?" But before I have a chance, the doorbell rings again.

This time, Mom answers the door and the Jackson-Browns walk in. They're like a whirlwind of perfectness sweeping through our living room.

Dr. and Mrs. Jackson-Brown are super friendly. They say we should all call them Edward and Kate, even the kids. Edward gives Max and me a big box of candy. Kate gives Mom a big bunch of flowers tied with a ribbon.

Chloe Jennifer looks like she just stepped out of a fashion magazine.

Everyone acts like they think everything about the Jackson-Browns is great. Even Winnie, who never thinks anything is great, says she loves Chloe Jennifer's outfit.

When we sit down for dinner, things go from bad to worse.

Chloe Jennifer says she loves Mary Ann's *Fashion Rocks* T-shirt.

Mary Ann smiles like she likes hearing that.

Chloe Jennifer says that she saw Joey skateboarding and that he's really good.

Joey smiles like he likes hearing that.

Chloe Jennifer says she thinks Winnie has cool style.

Winnie smiles like she likes hearing that.

Chloe Jennifer says that she noticed a piano in our living room and that she's been playing since she was five.

Mom smiles like she likes hearing that. She tells Chloe Jennifer that she's the music teacher at Fern Falls Elementary and that she would love to hear Chloe Jennifer play the piano after dinner.

Once everyone finishes eating, Chloe Jennifer takes her plate to the sink while Mom clears the table. "What a helpful guest," Mom says to her. Then we all go to the living room and listen to Chloe Jennifer play her favorite piece on the piano.

When she's finished, everyone claps. "Bravo," says Dad.

"You're quite a musician," says Mom.

When I learned to play the tuba, I don't remember Mom saying that I was "quite a musician."

It's like someone turned on the TV and we're watching the Chloe Jennifer show and everyone likes what they're seeing.

Even Champ goes over to Chloe Jennifer and gives her a big, sloppy lick. Chloe Jennifer bends down and gives Champ a big hug around the neck. "I love dogs," she says to everyone. "I've always wanted one, but I can't get Mom and Dad to say yes."

Kate laughs. "We're just waiting for the right moment," she says.

Chloe Jennifer sighs. I can tell she's been waiting a long time for this "right moment" to happen.

Chloe Jennifer's dad clears his throat like it's time to change the subject.

"We can't get over how much you two girls look alike," he says, motioning to Mary Ann and Chloe Jennifer.

"No one is going to believe it when we go to school on Monday," says Mary Ann.

SCHOOL! I hadn't even thought about

what it will be like when Chloe Jennifer comes to school. It will be just like this dinner but worse. This dinner was just one night. That will be every day!

Chloe Jennifer looks down at her boots. "I'm really scared to go to a new school."

"Don't worry," says Mary Ann. "Mallory and I walk to school together every day. You can walk with us. Once we get to school, we'll introduce you to everybody. You can sit with us at lunch and hang out with us at recess. We'll be a threesome." She looks at me. "Right, Mallory?"

I try to swallow, but I feel like there's a cement truck stuck in my throat.

I feel bad that Chloe Jennifer is scared to go to a new school. But I also don't feel good about being a threesome with Mary Ann and Chloe Jennifer. Mary Ann has always been my best friend, and the truth is that I don't like the idea of someone else being best friends with us.

Mary Ann clears her throat. "Right, Mallory?" she says again.

"Right," I say, because I know there's really nothing else I can say. But if you ask me, this all feels wrong.

A SWITCH-UP

I try not to frown as I cross the yard between my house and Mary Ann's house. Mary Ann and Chloe Jennifer are already standing outside and talking. Chloe Jennifer is laughing at whatever Mary Ann just said.

"Hi, Mallory!" says Chloe Jennifer like she's really happy to see me.

"Hi!" I try to sound like I'm just as happy to see her, but the truth is, it feels weird to be walking to school with Mary Ann *and*

Chloe Jennifer. I usually just walk with Mary Ann. Joey used to walk with us, but lately he's been going early to play soccer with some of the other boys.

Mary Ann links one arm through mine and the other through Chloe Jennifer's. "We're off to Fern Falls Elementary!" says Mary Ann, like she's Dorothy from *The Wizard of Oz* and we're the Scarecrow and the Tin Man.

I adjust the strap on my backpack and try not to think about what Mary Ann said about us all being a "threesome."

"So what do I need to know for my first day?" Chloe Jennifer asks.

Mary Ann tells Chloe Jennifer that our teacher, Mr. Knight, doesn't like to be interrupted.

She says that our PE teacher, Coach Kelly, makes us do push-ups and sit-ups.

She says that Chloe Jennifer should NOT eat the meatloaf in the cafeteria. Mary Ann makes a face like just the thought of eating it makes her want to barf.

Chloe Jennifer laughs. "You're so funny," she says to Mary Ann.

Chloe Jennifer might be laughing, but I'm not. I can tell that Mary Ann is trying really hard to make Chloe Jennifer like her. And she wouldn't do that unless she really liked Chloe Jennifer. I'm supposed to be Mary Ann's best friend, but I'm starting to feel like Mary Ann wants more than one best friend.

When we get to our classroom, Mr. Knight is expecting Chloe Jennifer. After the bell rings, he introduces her to everyone. Then he says it's time to work on our science projects. "Please find your partners."

I smile when he says that. Mary Ann and I are science project partners. We're almost done with our food chain report. Mary Ann and I push our desks together, and I pull out my folder with all of our notes.

Then Chloe Jennifer raises her hand. "Mr. Knight, I don't have a science project partner," she says.

Mr. Knight smacks his forehead like hes can't believe he didn't think of that. "Who would like to volunteer to let Chloe Jennifer be part of their project?" he asks.

Lots of hands go up, but one hand is higher than all the others.

"Thank you, Mary Ann," says Mr. Knight. "Chloe Jennifer can work with you and Mallory."

Chloe Jennifer pulls her desk up to ours. I listen while Mary Ann starts explaining our project to Chloe Jennifer.

"We'll have to change it a little bit now that you're working with us," says Mary Ann. "But that won't be too hard. And it'll be more fun that way anyway."

I try not to look upset, but I think our report is fun enough the way it is. Mary Ann and I have already decided exactly how we're going to do this project, and I liked our plan. Now Mary Ann starts crossing off a bunch of our ideas and writing down new ones that Chloe Jennifer can help us with. And she doesn't even ask what *I* want to do.

When the lunch bell rings, I race to the cafeteria. Lunch is one of the best parts of the day. But when I get to my table, lunch doesn't start off any better than the morning did.

All the girls in my class want to sit by Chloe Jennifer and talk to her. Arielle and Danielle slide over to make room for her, but Mary Ann grabs Chloe Jennifer's arm like she's the one in charge of her.

"Chloe Jennifer is going to sit between

Mallory and me," she says. Then she tells me to scoot over so Chloe Jennifer can squeeze in between us.

I scoot over, but not because I want to. When everyone sits down, the only thing anyone is talking about is how much Chloe Jennifer looks like Mary Ann.

"It's so weird!" says Grace.

"You look like sisters," says Emma.

"Not just sisters—they look like twins!" says Dawn.

I don't say a word—because if I did, what I'd say is that I'm tired of hearing about how much Chloe Jennifer and Mary Ann look alike. I'm tired of talking about Chloe Jennifer—period. But no one else is.

"Where are you from?" asks Pamela.

"What do you like to do?" asks April.

"I love your dress," says Arielle.

"Me too!" says Danielle.

Chloe Jennifer tells everyone about her life back in Atlanta and how she loves to dance, play piano, and shop. "I also like peanut butter and marshmallow sandwiches. That's what I have for lunch every day."

"That's Mallory's favorite sandwich too!"

says Mary Ann. "Her mom always packs one for her."

Chloe Jennifer smiles at me. "We can be sandwich buddies," she says. But when she opens her lunch bag, she stops smiling.

"What's the matter?" asks Mary Ann.

Chloe Jennifer pulls a little note out of her lunch bag and starts reading.

Chloe Jennifer takes out her sandwich and peeks between the bread slices.

"What is it?" asks Zoe.

My dearest daughter,

I could not find the marshmallow creme. It must have gotten lost in the move! I will go grocery shopping today and get some so that tomorrow you can take your favorite sandwich in your lunch. I hope you have a great first day of school!

Love, Mom

"Bologna and cheese," says Chloe Jennifer.

"Ewww!" says Arielle. Lots of other girls start ewww-ing, including me. April puts her hands on her throat and sticks her tongue out like just the thought of it makes her want to gag.

"It's so sad that you can't have a sandwich you like on your first day at a new school," says Brittany.

"It's no big deal," says Chloe Jennifer. But it's easy to see that she's disappointed.

Mary Ann shakes her head. "We have to do something about this," she says. Then she snaps her fingers like she just came up with the perfect solution.

"Mallory, you give Chloe Jennifer half of your sandwich, and you can take half of hers. Then you'll both have something you like."

Mary Ann smiles at Chloe Jennifer.

"Mallory and I always share sandwiches," she says.

"What a great idea!" says Arielle.

"Are you sure you don't mind?" asks Chloe Jennifer.

"Of course she doesn't mind," says Mary Ann. She gives me a *time-to-hand-over-half-your-sandwich* look.

I don't want to hand over half my sandwich, but all the other girls are looking at me, and I can tell they expect me to share.

I reach over and place half of my delicious-looking peanut butter and marshmallow sandwich in front of Chloe Jennifer.

Chloe Jennifer smiles and puts half of her disgusting-looking bologna and cheese in front of me. "Thanks, Mallory," she says. She takes a bite. "Mmm! This is great."

I nod like I'm happy she's happy.

But that's not really the case.

Even though I know this was just a sandwich switch-up, it feels more like a best friend switch-up. How could Mary Ann offer half of my sandwich to a girl she barely knows?

It seems like Mary Ann cares more about how Chloe Jennifer feels than how I feel. How I feel right now is sick to my stomach.

And I haven't even had a bite of Chloe Jennifer's sandwich.

HERE, THERE, EVERYWHERE

Mary Ann has gone crazy! Chloe-Jennifer-Jackson-Brown-crazy!

Ever since the Jackson-Brown family moved to Wish Pond Road, Mary Ann has made Chloe Jennifer a part of everything we do. No matter what I try to do with Mary Ann, she includes Chloe Jennifer too. I feel like I barely have a best friend anymore.

Last night, Grandma called and I tried to tell her what's going on, but she wasn't much help. All she had to say is that in her opinion, three's company. But if you ask me, she got it all wrong! Three's not company. Three's a crowd, and I don't like it!

Stuff I didn't like happened all week at school, and it happened this weekend too. If you don't believe me, keep reading and you'll see what I mean.

TUESDAY

Tuesday at recess, I got my friends to play Purple Dot Jinx. I love to play Purple Dot Jinx, and so does Mary Ann. We made up the game, and we're really good at it.

When you play, someone asks a question like, "What's your favorite food?" If two people say the same answer, they scream "Purple dot jinx!" at the same time and they each get a point. Mary Ann and I know each other so well that we always answer the same, which means we always get lots of points.

But this time, Mary Ann taught Chloe Jennifer how the game works, and when we played, Chloe Jennifer kept yelling a lot of the same answers that Mary Ann and I were yelling.

When I saw what was happening, I said maybe we should play a different game, but Mary Ann said that I was the one who wanted to play this game, and then she said how much she loves that there's another girl who has all the same answers we have.

She might love it, but I don't.

WEDNESDAY

On Wednesday morning, I called Mary Ann and said we should wear our new purple glittery sweaters that we bought last week. Mary Ann thought that was a great idea, so we both wore our purple glittery sweaters to school.

But guess what? Chloe Jennifer was wearing the same sweater!

Earlier in the week, Mary Ann had told her about our matching sweaters, and Chloe Jennifer's mom had bought her one too!

And to make things worse, no one talked

about how Mary Ann and I looked in our matching sweaters. All anyone talked about was how much Mary Ann and Chloe Jennifer looked alike in *their* matching sweaters.

I'm not just talking about the kids in my class. I'm talking about everybody at school.

During morning assembly, a group of third-graders asked if they were twins.

When our principal, Mrs. Finney, came to our classroom to make an announcement, she made a comment about how much they look alike.

During art, Mrs. Pearl said that seeing them had given her an idea for an art project. She told everyone that we were going to practice drawing two things that look the same.

And at lunch, a bunch of fifth-grade girls came over to our table. One of them used her phone to take a picture of Mary Ann and Chloe Jennifer. She said she was going to submit it to a look-alike contest.

Arielle and Danielle thought it was cool that fifth-grade girls, who never come over to our lunch table, came over to our lunch table.

I didn't think anything about it was cool.

THURSDAY

On Thursday, we presented our science projects in class.

Before Chloe Jennifer joined our group, Mary Ann and I had decided I would read the part of our report about plants, which are producers, and Mary Ann would read the part about animals, which are consumers.

But when Chloe Jennifer joined our group, Mary Ann said that she and Chloe Jennifer could do the consumer part together, and that instead of just reading the parts, we should act them out.

So that's what we did. I acted like a plant, and Mary Ann and Chloe Jennifer acted like animals that eat plants.

When they pretended to eat me, everybody in my class was laughing.

But they weren't laughing because I was funny. They were laughing because Mary Ann and Chloe Jennifer were funny together. All I did was stand there and get eaten.

To me, it wasn't funny at all.

FRIDAY

Friday after school, I asked Mom if she would take Mary Ann and me to the mall.

We love to go to the mall, and we love to eat cinnamon sugar pretzels there. I was already picturing us sitting on the bench in the food court, eating our pretzels.

Mom said she would be happy to take us. So I called Mary Ann and invited her, and Mary Ann said she would call Chloe Jennifer and see if she wanted to go too.

I tried to tell Mary Ann that Chloe Jennifer wouldn't want to go the mall with us because we're going to eat cinnamon sugar pretzels and not everybody likes cinnamon sugar pretzels.

But Mary Ann said she would ask Chloe Jennifer if she likes them.

Chloe Jennifer said that she likes cinnamon sugar pretzels but that she likes frozen yogurt with strawberries even more. Mary Ann said that sounded delicious and that we should try it.

So, instead of going to the mall with Mary Ann and eating cinnamon sugar pretzels, I went to the mall with Mary Ann AND Chloe Jennifer and ate frozen yogurt with strawberries, which was NOT what I wanted to be doing!

Even though the frozen yogurt with strawberries did taste pretty good.

SATURDAY

Saturday morning, I went over to watch *Fashion Fran* at Mary Ann's house. But guess who was already there?

If you guessed Chloe Jennifer, you guessed right.

When *Fashion Fran* was over, I said, "Well, we'd *all* better be going home now." I gave Mary Ann my best *you-should-tell-Chloe-Jennifer-to-go-home-so-we-can-spend-the-rest-of-the-day-together-like-we-always-do* look.

I was sure Mary Ann would catch on and tell Chloe Jennifer to go home. But all Mary Ann said was, "Why don't you and Chloe Jennifer stay for lunch? Then we can help Chloe Jennifer plan her birthday party."

Before I could say anything, Chloe Jennifer was jumping up and down and clapping. So Mary Ann and I spent the day Saturday helping Chloe Jennifer plan her party.

Saturdays are supposed to be the day I spend with my best friend, NOT the day I spend with my best friend and a new girl.

Now it's Sunday night. I'm curled up on my bed with Cheeseburger and rubbing the fur behind her ears. I think about what it's been like since Chloe Jennifer moved to Wish Pond Road.

Mary Ann really likes her.

It's not that I don't. I just don't like that having her around makes everything with Mary Ann different. It's like Mary Ann has forgotten that we're supposed to be best friends.

It's never just the two of us anymore. It's always the three of us. And it seems like Mary Ann likes it that way.

I pretend I'm at the wish pond. I close my eyes and make a wish.

I wish things could go back to being like they were with Mary Ann before Chloe Jennifer Jackson-Brown moved here.

I open my eyes, but when I do, I know the wish I made is one that won't come true. Things can't go back to how they were.

But there's got to be a way to show Mary Ann that being a threesome doesn't work. I've got to remind her how much fun we have when we do things together—just the two of us!

I close my eyes again to try to think of something.

When I do, an idea pops into my head. I don't know why I didn't think of it before.

"I'm going to stop being part of this threesome. If I do that, Mary Ann will realize she misses being best friends with me and that she'd rather be my friend than Chloe Jennifer's best friend," I say to my cat.

I look at Cheeseburger to see if she gets it.

She purrs. I'm not sure if her purr means she gets it or not.

But I *am* sure of one thing. Operation *Three's a Crowd* begins first thing tomorrow morning.

OPERATION THREE'S A CROWD

As soon as I leave for school, I put my plan into action.

"Are you ready for the science test?" Chloe Jennifer asks Mary Ann and me as we walk to school. "Did you study? Do you think it will be hard?"

Chloe Jennifer always asks Mary Ann

and me lots of questions when we walk to school. Usually, I answer those questions. But today I don't say anything.

Mary Ann nods that she's ready and looks at me. "Do you know the different types of clouds?" she asks.

I just shrug. I'm not going to say anything on the subject of clouds—or on any other subject.

While Mary Ann and Chloe Jennifer talk about the difference between stratus clouds and cirrus clouds, I slow down.

When they get a few feet ahead of me, Mary Ann turns around and gives me a *what-are-you-doing?* look. "Mallory, aren't you coming?" she asks.

"There's not enough room on the sidewalk for three people to walk together," I say to Mary Ann, like I'm explaining something obvious.

Mary Ann looks down at the sidewalk, and then she looks at me again. I don't know if her look means she thinks there is enough room for three people to walk together on the sidewalk or if it means she doesn't like that I'm not walking with them. What I do know is that if I want Mary Ann to be my best friend again, I have to continue Operation *Three's a Crowd.*

At lunch, that's exactly what I do.

When Chloe Jennifer sits down between Mary Ann and me, which is where she's been sitting every day since she got to Fern Falls Elementary, I open my lunch bag and take out my Oreos.

Mary Ann smiles when she sees them. She loves Oreos as much as I do, and I always share mine with her.

But today, I don't share my Oreos with anybody. I put my stack of cookies out on a napkin in front of me. Then, when I'm done eating my sandwich and apple, I pick up a cookie and take apart the two sides. "Mmmm," I say as I take a bite.

Mary Ann smiles at me. "I'm ready for my cookies too," she says.

I look over at Chloe Jennifer. Then I look back at Mary Ann. "Sorry," I say. "I don't have enough for all three of us, and I wouldn't want to leave anyone out."

I don't like not sharing my cookies, but I have to make a point. I have to get Mary Ann to realize that three people can't be best friends.

Tastes better when shared ♡ with FRIENDS. ♡

Mary Ann wrinkles her nose like something smells funny, and it's not just the cafeteria's fish sticks. I shrug and take another bite.

Mary Ann looks at me like she'd really like a cookie. I'd really like Mary Ann to be my best friend again.

After school, I keep Operation *Three's a Crowd* going.

"Do you want to study our spelling words together?" Chloe Jennifer asks Mary Ann and me when we're almost home.

Mary Ann says that would be great. I don't like what I'm about to say, but I don't feel like I have a choice. I tell them they can do it together without me. "Studying spelling words is easier with two people than with three people," I say.

Mary Ann gives me a *we-always-study-our-spelling-words-together* look. But before she can say anything else, I wave good-bye and walk into my house.

When I get inside, I go to my room and close my door.

"Day One of Operation *Three's a Crowd* was a success," I tell Cheeseburger.

Well, it was mostly a success.

A BEST FRIEND REUNION

Mallory, where are you? | I'm right here!

Happiness again! | Best friends Forever!

Part of me feels like this is the only way I can get Mary Ann to remember how much fun we used to have when it was just the two of us, so that she'll want to be my best friend again. But another part of me misses doing things like talking about science tests and sharing Oreos and studying spelling words.

I rub the fur behind Cheeseburger's ears. "I hope this plan won't take too long to work," I tell my cat.

The next morning, I put Operation *Three's a Crowd* back into action.

I don't walk with Mary Ann and Chloe Jennifer on the way to school.

I don't offer to help them when they're trying to decide what kind of cake Chloe Jennifer is going to have at her birthday party.

And I tell them I don't want to play Chinese jump rope after school, even though they remind me that it takes three people to play it.

I keep my plan going all week.

Even though Mary Ann hasn't said anything yet, I can tell she knows something is different. I know Mary Ann better than anybody, and I know that soon she'll say we need to talk.

When we talk, I know she'll say something like, *Mallory, things have been really, really, really weird between us since Chloe Jennifer moved to Wish Pond Road. It's too hard for three people to be best friends. Let's just keep things the way they've always been.*

Then we'll hug and pinky swear to always be lifelong best friends. Things will be just like they used to be. Thinking about it makes me smile.

I just hope I don't have to wait too long for Mary Ann to say she wants to have this talk, because it's not much fun doing everything alone.

The good news is that I don't have to wait long at all.

Thursday after school, Mary Ann calls me to see if she can come over. "We need to talk," she says.

"Great!" I say into the phone. I can hardly wait for her to get here!

"Operation *Three's a Crowd* worked!" I say to Cheeseburger.

When Mary Ann gets to my house, I hook my arm through hers. I practically drag her to my bedroom.

Mary Ann starts talking the minute she sits down on my bed. "Mallory, we have a problem."

"I agree," I tell her.

"It's Chloe Jennifer," says Mary Ann.
I nod.

Mary Ann looks like what she's about to say next is important.

I know this is the part where Mary Ann is going to say that it's too hard for three people to be best friends and that we should just go back to how things were before Chloe Jennifer got here.

I lean toward Mary Ann. I don't want to miss a word she's about to say.

Mary Ann clears her throat. "The problem is that Chloe Jennifer thinks you don't like her. You haven't exactly been acting like you want to hang out with her. And that's not OK. We all live on the same street, and she's really nice." Mary Ann shrugs, like it's as simple as that. "We should all be friends."

She pauses, and I can tell she expects me to say something now. I take a deep breath. But the truth is, I have no idea

what to say. This talk is not going the way I expected at all.

Mary Ann and I just sit on my bed for a long time, not saying anything to each other.

Finally, Mary Ann breaks the silence. "Mallory, why don't we have a sleepover at your house this weekend?"

I let out a huge sigh of relief. "Sure," I say. We have sleepovers almost every weekend, and lots of times we have them at my house. This will be a perfect chance to start acting like best friends again. My plan must have worked after all!

"Great!" says Mary Ann. "I think you should invite Chloe Jennifer. That will show her that you like her. What do you think?"

What I think is that Mary Ann is the one who needs to do some thinking! "Why can't it just be the two of us?" I ask. "Since we're best friends . . ."

Mary Ann shakes her head like we're practicing a really easy spelling word and I keep getting it wrong. "Mallory, of course we're best friends. But we can be friends with other people too. You know what I mean?"

I nod like I get it, but I don't. We've always had other friends, but never other friends who go everywhere we go and do everything we do.

Mary Ann smiles. "Great!"

Then she raises her right hand and holds up her pinky. "Pinky swear that you'll invite Chloe Jennifer to our sleepover this weekend and show her that you like her."

I look at Mary Ann, but I don't move.

She didn't say anything about how I didn't do stuff with her this week. Not one word about how she missed walking to school or sharing my cookies or studying our spelling words or playing together. Everything she's said since she came over has been about Chloe Jennifer.

I reach across my bed and pull Cheeseburger into my lap. Operation *Three's a Crowd* has only made things worse.

Mary Ann gives me a *time-to-start-pinky-swearing* look. Slowly, I raise my right arm and hook my pinky around Mary Ann's.

When I do, she grins.

But only one of us is smiling.

THE SLEEPOVER

It's not New Year's Eve, but I make a resolution anyway. I'm going to try to be friends with Chloe Jennifer.

When I invited her to the sleepover, she gave me a big hug and told me how excited she is to come. Mary Ann was right about one thing . . . Chloe Jennifer is really nice. Maybe the three of us being friends won't be so bad.

Plus, I don't see how I can NOT be friends

with Chloe Jennifer. If Mary Ann is friends with her and I'm not, that means they would just be friends with each other. I don't want Mary Ann to decide that she's having so much fun being friends with Chloe Jennifer that she doesn't even miss being friends with me.

Just thinking about that makes me realize how much I DON'T want that to happen.

What I do want is to make this sleepover extra amazing. I have lots of fun stuff planned for tonight.

As soon as I hear the doorbell, I race down the hall to answer it. When I open the door, Mary Ann and Chloe Jennifer are standing there with their sleeping bags and backpacks.

"Welcome to the world's greatest slumber party!" I say. I hand each of them a copy of the schedule I wrote out.

We head to my room, but before I can show Chloe Jennifer where to put her stuff, Mary Ann says, "Just leave it anywhere on the floor."

While Chloe Jennifer puts her stuff in the corner, Mary Ann dumps her sleeping bag and backpack in the middle of the room. Then she shoves the schedule I made in her back pocket. She doesn't even bother to look at it.

"OK," says Mary Ann. "We always bake cookies when we have a sleepover." She takes Chloe Jennifer's arm. "Let's go to the kitchen."

I follow my friends down the hall, but I don't like how Mary Ann is acting. This sleepover is at *my* house.

When we get to the kitchen, Mom is already there.

"Your junior chefs have arrived!" Mary Ann says to Mom. She starts pointing to

85

cabinets and drawers, telling Chloe Jennifer where we keep everything.

"You are certainly a helpful junior chef, Mary Ann," Mom laughs.

I don't see anything funny about this. Maybe Mary Ann knows where we keep everything in my kitchen, but it doesn't mean she's the one who gets to show Chloe Jennifer.

Mom helps us mix the dough. When we're done, Mary Ann gives Chloe Jennifer a spoon. "Since you're the guest, you get to put the dough on the cookie sheets."

I give Mary Ann a *who-made-you-the-boss?* look. But Mary Ann doesn't pay any attention.

Once the cookies are in the oven, Mary Ann says, "Time to get the lemonade and popcorn ready. We're going to watch a movie now."

I wrinkle my nose. I love the smell of cookies baking, but I don't like how Mary Ann is acting like this is *her* sleepover.

We watch a movie and have popcorn and lemonade and cookies. When the movie is over, I put my copy of the schedule on the table so Mary Ann and Chloe Jennifer can see it.

"Now it's time to go to the wish pond," I say. "Joey said he would meet us outside and teach us some skateboard tricks."

Mary Ann pretend-yawns like that's the most boring idea she's heard in a long time. "Why don't we go to your room and make up a dance?" She looks at Chloe Jennifer. "Since we're both dancers, I'll bet

we could come up with something really good. That'll be so much fun!"

I give Mary Ann a *since-I'm-not-a-dancer-that-doesn't-sound-like-fun-to-me* look.

"I don't know," says Chloe Jennifer. "Mallory might not want to do that."

I'm a little surprised to hear her say that. It's kind of like she's a mind-reader and she can guess what I'm thinking but not saying.

But Mary Ann is already heading toward my room. "We'll teach Mallory what to do," she says over her shoulder.

Chloe Jennifer looks at me. "Is that OK?" she asks.

I shrug like it's fine, but it's not. I spent a lot of time planning this sleepover. I really don't like how Mary Ann is taking over.

By the time Chloe Jennifer and I get to my room, Mary Ann is already looking through the pile of CDs on my desk. "First, we need to find some good music for our dance," she says. She picks up a CD case and points to one of the songs listed on the back. "What do you think of this one?" she asks Chloe Jennifer, like her opinion is the only one in this room that counts.

"I guess it's OK," she says. She looks at me like she wants to make sure I like the song too.

I lean over Mary Ann's shoulder to see which song she's talking about. "I don't like that song," I say. I cross my arms across my chest. "And I don't want to dance to it."

Mary Ann looks at me and snaps her fingers like I just gave her a great idea. "Mallory, since you don't like this song and you don't really know how to dance, Chloe Jennifer and I will do the dance and you can be our stylist."

Before I can say if I want to do that or not, Mary Ann says, "We're going to need costumes." She starts looking though my costume box and takes out the matching cheerleader costumes we wore last Halloween.

She hands one of them to Chloe Jennifer. "We can both be cheerleaders. Since we look alike, we should dress alike too. This will be the coolest dance ever! We're going to have so much fun!"

I can't believe what I'm hearing. Does Mary Ann really think I will have fun being the stylist while she and Chloe Jennifer do a look-alike cheerleader dance that doesn't include me?

Best Used when there's something to cheer about!

Chloe Jennifer starts putting on the cheerleader costume, but she looks like she's not sure if she should be excited about this plan either.

When Mary Ann and Chloe Jennifer both have their costumes on, Mary Ann looks at their reflection in the mirror. "We have a problem," she says.

For the first time today, I agree with Mary Ann. We definitely have a problem!

"Our hair and makeup need to be the same if we're going to look alike," says Mary Ann. "Mallory, since you're the stylist, that's your job!"

Mary Ann goes into the bathroom and brings back some of my purple eye shadow and pink lip gloss. She hands them to me and gives me a *time-to-work-your-styling-magic* look.

Even though I usually love doing people's hair and makeup, I don't want to be the stylist today. But I feel like if I say so, Mary Ann is going to say I'm ruining the coolest dance ever.

I open the container of eye shadow and start rubbing purple glitter shadow on Mary Ann's lids. Then I put pink sparkle gloss on her lips.

"Isn't this fun?" says Mary Ann when I'm done with her makeup. I don't say anything. Neither does Chloe Jennifer.

I start to put the purple glitter shadow on Chloe Jennifer's lids, but she stops me. "You don't have to do my makeup," she says.

Mary Ann shakes her head. "Of course she does! We can't do a look-alike dance if we don't look alike. And it's the stylist's job to make sure we look alike."

Chloe Jennifer looks at me like she doesn't like how Mary Ann is acting any more than I do.

I'm trying to have a good attitude about this sleepover, but Mary Ann isn't making it easy. I feel like she doesn't care if I'm having fun or not.

"OK, now we need to do our hair the same," says Mary Ann. She opens one of my drawers and hands me a brush, some ponytail holders, and four red ribbons. "Mallory, can you give us both pigtails with ribbons?"

I feel like Cinderella dressing her stepsisters for the ball. No one cared if she went to the ball, and no one cares if I'm part of this dance.

I start brushing Mary Ann's hair. I brush her hair into two high pigtails. When I'm done, I tie red ribbons around each one of her pigtails.

"OK, now it's Chloe Jennifer's turn," says Mary Ann.

Chloe Jennifer sits in front of my mirror. She tries to smile, but if you ask me, it's more of a pretend smile than a real smile.

I make pigtails on each side of her head, and then I tie red ribbons around each one.

When I'm done, Mary Ann sticks her face next to Chloe Jennifer's in the mirror.

Then she frowns. "We still don't look exactly alike, because your pigtails are longer than mine," she says to Chloe Jennifer.

I shake my head and give Mary Ann a *this-look-alike-thing-is-getting-old* look.

But Mary Ann isn't paying attention to me. "We should trim Chloe Jennifer's pigtails," she says.

Chloe Jennifer's pretend-smile disappears.

Mary Ann doesn't seem to notice. She finds the scissors on my desk and hands them to me. "Mallory, just trim a little off each of Chloe Jennifer's pigtails."

"I don't think we need to do that," says Chloe Jennifer.

"I do," says Mary Ann. "It's the only way to really be look-alikes."

I put the scissors down on my dresser and cross my arms. "I don't want to cut Chloe Jennifer's hair," I say.

Mary Ann lets out a loud breath like this is taking way too long. She picks the scissors up and shoves them into my hand. "Start cutting!"

I look at Mary Ann's reflection in the mirror. Mary Ann can be bossy, but she's never *this* bossy.

She's obsessed with being a look-alike with Chloe Jennifer. And I think I know why. I was right—three people can't all be best friends. There can only be two best friends, and Mary Ann wants to be best friends with Chloe Jennifer. Not with me.

"C'mon, Mallory!" says Mary Ann.

I really can't believe how Mary Ann is acting. It's almost like she's daring me to cut Chloe Jennifer's hair. I keep staring at her in the mirror and give her a *your-dare-doesn't-scare-me* look.

Then I pick up Chloe Jennifer's pigtail and start cutting.

SCISSOR (UN)HAPPY

"Mallory, look what you did!" Mary Ann's words are barely a whisper, but they sound scarier than if she had yelled at the tops of her lungs.

I look down at the floor. There's blonde hair everywhere.

One minute, Mary Ann was telling me to hurry up and cut Chloe Jennifer's hair so they could be look-alikes, and the next minute, the scissors in my hand cut off Chloe Jennifer's whole pigtail.

I look at Chloe Jennifer. In third grade, my teacher Mrs. Daily taught us the expression *white as a ghost*. Now I know exactly what it means.

Chloe Jennifer looks at herself in the mirror. On one side of her head, there's a long, blonde, curly pigtail. On the other side of her head, there's only a little, short pigtail and a big red bow.

Chloe Jennifer reaches up and puts her hand on the side of her head where her pigtail used to be.

"I'm so sorry. It was an accident," I say. I hear the words coming out of my mouth, but the voice saying them doesn't sound like mine.

I look at Chloe Jennifer to see if she believes me. But she looks like she's too

shocked to know what she believes. A tear rolls down her cheek.

My room feels too hot. I don't know how this happened. I didn't mean to cut off her pigtail. It was like the scissors had a mind of their own.

"We have to get your mom," says Mary Ann. She's as red as Chloe Jennifer is white. And her voice is loud now. Too loud.

Everything that comes next is a blur.

Mom is in my room.

Chloe Jennifer's mom is in my room.

Chloe Jennifer is crying.

Mary Ann is telling them what happened.

They all look at Chloe Jennifer to see if she's OK. Then they all look at me like I'm a criminal.

I can feel big tears starting in the corners of my eyes.

I try to tell them that it was Mary Ann's idea for me to cut Chloe Jennifer's hair in the first place. I try to explain that I didn't want to cut her hair and that Mary Ann made me do it.

But no one seems to be listening.

"I'm so sorry," Mom says to Kate and Chloe Jennifer.

"I think it's time for us to go home," says Kate. She helps Chloe Jennifer get her things together. Then she wraps an arm around her daughter. Mom follows them out of my room.

Now it's just Mary Ann and me. We've been alone in my room hundreds of times, but this time, it feels different.

I start to say again that I didn't mean for this to happen, but Mary Ann holds up her hand, stop-sign style. "Mallory, you made a pinky swear that you would show Chloe Jennifer that you like her."

"I tried!" I tell her.

"By cutting off her pigtail?"

I feel like a stranger is standing in front of me, not my best friend. Mary Ann looks so mad. But I'm mad too. I'm not the only one who did something wrong. This is partly Mary Ann's fault.

Everything I'm feeling starts spilling out.

"I did try! I invited Chloe Jennifer to sleep over. I planned lots of fun stuff for the three of us to do—together—but you were acting like it was *your* sleepover and you only wanted to do things with her! You were the one who wanted to make up a dance. It was your idea for you and Chloe Jennifer to be cheerleader twins. And it was your idea for me to cut her hair!"

"I can't believe you're blaming me for this!" says Mary Ann. "You didn't want to invite Chloe Jennifer to our sleepover in the first place."

I look at the expression on Mary Ann's face. A minute ago, she just looked mad. Now she looks scared too. I know she doesn't want to admit that she had anything to do with what just happened. But she did. She had a lot to do with everything that's gone wrong, starting on the day Chloe Jennifer came to Wish Pond Road.

"Ever since Chloe Jennifer moved here, you've been acting like she's your best friend and not me!" I say.

"I was trying to be extra nice to Chloe Jennifer because you weren't being nice to her at all," says Mary Ann.

"I never meant to be NOT nice," I say. "But *we're* supposed to be best friends!"

Mary Ann folds her arms across her chest like she's tired of talking about this. "Mallory, you broke our pinky swear. I can't be best friends with someone who breaks pinky swears." She walks to the middle of my room and picks up her sleeping bag.

As hot as I was before, I'm just as cold now.

"What do you mean?" I ask.

Mary Ann swings her backpack onto her shoulder. "I mean that our friendship is over," she says.

I must have heard her wrong.

We're lifelong best friends. I open my mouth to tell Mary Ann that our lifelong best friendship can't be over. But before I can say a word, Mary Ann is gone.

ALL ALONE

By Poor Little Mallory McDonald

Once upon a time, there was a sweet, smart, cute (at least, that's what people told her) little girl with red hair and freckles who accidentally cut off another girl's pigtail. She didn't mean to do it, but she did it, and lots of people were upset about it.

Her parents were upset. Not only did they have a long talk with her about how disappointed they were in her, but they also told her she was grounded.

When she asked how long she was grounded for, all they said was that she should not make any plans ... FOR A VERY LONG TIME!

EXHIBIT A: UPSET PARENTS

Her brother was upset. His girlfriend said she was scared to come over, because if the little girl with red hair and freckles cut off another girl's pigtail, there's no telling what else she might cut off.

Her brother was angry that his girlfriend wouldn't come over, so he was hardly speaking to the poor little girl. He hardly spoke to her anyway, but ever since she cut off the girl's pigtail, he hadn't said anything to her except that she's a "whack job."

EXHIBIT B: GIRLFRIEND and BROTHER

The girl whose pigtail was cut off was upset. When the little girl with red hair and freckles called to say that she was sorry, the other girl said she wasn't mad—but the little girl with red hair and freckles couldn't help thinking that she was.

She thought this for two reasons.

Reason #1: The other girl was unusually quiet on the phone. She didn't ask any questions or get excited about things like she usually did.

Reason #2: She was missing a pigtail. The little girl with red hair and freckles couldn't help but think that if *she* was missing a pigtail, *she* would be mad.

EXHIBIT C:
Quiet + hairless (on one side) = MAD!!!

The other girl's parents were upset. The little girl with red hair and freckles apologized to them too, but they were even quieter than their daughter, and they never said that they weren't mad.

Another person who was upset was the lifelong best friend of the poor little girl with red hair and freckles. It had been almost a week since the little girl with red hair and freckles cut off the other girl's pigtail, and in that whole time, her best friend hadn't said one word to her. The last thing her best friend had said was that their friendship was over.

The little girl had tried several times to talk to her best friend, but her best friend would not listen to anything she tried to say.

The little girl missed her best friend. And, to be honest, she also missed the girl whose pigtail she'd accidentally cut off. She'd had her doubts about

this girl, but the more she'd gotten to know her, the more she liked her. Now that she really thought about it, she knew she'd rather be friends with her than NOT be friends with her.

And to make matters worse (yes, even worse than they already were), lots of kids at school were also upset about what happened. In the opinion of the poor little girl, these kids shouldn't have been upset. They weren't even there when the other girl's pigtail got cut off.

But they were at school on the Monday morning after it happened, when the other girl came to school with a new, short haircut.

The lifelong best friend of the girl with red hair and freckles told everyone that there had been an "incident"

THE haircut that caused everyone to STOP Speaking to the poor little girl with red hair and freckles.

and that because of the "incident," the girl whose pigtail had been cut off had no choice but to cut off the rest of her hair. This made the other girls in the class ask lots more questions, and the answers to those questions made them upset.

They were upset even though the girl with the new haircut told them it was "no big deal." She said that she had always wanted to get a short haircut and actually liked the way it looked. But the rest of the kids were still mad at the poor little girl with red hair and freckles.

Worst of all, the girl with the new haircut told all the girls in the class that she was having a birthday party this weekend and that everyone was invited.

The poor little girl with red hair and freckles said that she was grounded, but that maybe her parents would let her go to the party anyway.

As soon as she said that, some of the girls in the class crossed their arms and rolled their eyes and looked at the poor little girl like she shouldn't even consider coming to the party.

This made the little girl sad. But when she looked at the girl with the new, short haircut, she felt even sadder. She had to wonder if . . .

A. The other girl really wanted her to come to her party.

OR

B. The other girl would be happier if she wasn't there at all.

And the more she thought about it, the more she thought that the answer was B.

This made the little girl feel terribly alone.

She's alone today. She's alone in her room where she's writing this story.

And she's going to be alone tomorrow. Tomorrow, all of her friends will be at the birthday party of the little girl whose pigtail she cut off, but she won't be there.

POOR, Sad, Lonely girl.

While her friends are painting pottery and eating cake, she'll be at home.

All alone.

PLANNING TIME

I put down my pad of paper and throw a rock into the wish pond. Whenever something goes wrong, the wish pond is where I come to think about how to fix things.

I watch the rock sink below the surface of the water. Then I throw another rock.

I think of all the times Dad has come out to the wish pond and sat and talked to me when I was upset. He usually knows just

the right thing to say. And he always tries to help me think of something I can do to make a bad situation better.

I really wish Dad was here right now.

But he's not. I'm not sure he would even know what to say this time. Since I cut off Chloe Jennifer's pigtail, Mom and Dad have spent a lot of time talking to me about how important it is to take responsibility for my actions. But they haven't actually told me how to do that.

Now, it's just me, and I have to think of a way to make things better on my own.

I think back to the day of the sleepover.

Even though Mary Ann was not acting like a good friend, I'm the one who cut off Chloe Jennifer's pigtail. And even though Chloe Jennifer told me that she's not mad and that she likes her haircut, I know what I did was wrong. I also know cutting off

Chloe Jennifer's pigtail wasn't the only thing I did wrong.

From the minute she moved to Wish Pond Road, I was so worried that she would mess up my friendship with Mary Ann that I didn't really give her a chance.

I have to think of a way to show everyone how sorry I am about the way I acted. I have to show Mary Ann that I want us to be best friends again. And I have to show Chloe Jennifer that I want to be friends with her too.

Think, Mallory.

I pick up a handful of rocks and start throwing them into the wish pond, one rock at a time. I make a wish that throwing rocks will help me think.

I close my eyes and make my brain think as hard as it has ever thought.

And then I, Mallory McDonald, think of

an absolutely great plan to make up for what I did.

I'm not sure I can get the plan to work. But I know I have to try.

Here's the problem. There are a lot of parts to my plan, and it won't work unless I can get every part done. And here's the other problem: I don't have much time to do it.

I look at my watch. Then I pick up my notebook and start making a checklist of all the things I have to do for my plan to work.

Getting all this done won't be easy, especially the *talking-to-Chloe-Jennifer's-mom-and-dad* part. The only thing I've said to them since the day I cut off Chloe Jennifer's pigtail is how sorry I was that I cut it off. They were still pretty mad then. I don't blame them. I just hope they'll listen to what I have to say.

{TO·DO LIST}

- ☐ Talk to mom.
- ☐ Talk to dad.
- ☐ Get them to unground me (at least for tomorrow).
- ☐ Clean out cars.
- ☐ Iron pajamas.
- ☐ Go to grocery store.
- ☐ Go to party store.
- ☐ Make decorations.
- ☐ Set up table.
- ☐ Make phone calls.
- ☐ Swear everyone I call to secrecy.
- ☐ Talk to Chloe Jennifer's mom and dad.

Tomorrow is Chloe Jennifer's birthday, and I really want to make it extra special.

Even though I have a lot to do and not much time to do it, I pick up another rock and close my eyes. I have one more wish to make. I really, really, really want this one to come true.

I wish my plan will work.

Now all I have to do is follow my list and set my alarm for tomorrow morning at 6 a.m. Sharp!

WAKE-UPS AND MAKEUPS

When my alarm goes off, I spring into action. It's only 6 a.m., but it's party time!

Before I even get out of bed, Mom is in my room. She's still in her nightgown. "Kitchen in five?" she asks.

I nod. It won't take me long to get dressed. In fact, it won't take me any time at all. For today's party, I'm staying in my pj's.

I get out of bed and give Mom a big hug. "Thanks for ungrounding me," I say. "And for helping me with my plan."

Mom wraps an arm around me and gives me a *growing-up-isn't-always-easy* look. "I'm glad to see that you're taking responsibility for your actions," she says. "And I love your idea! I think Chloe Jennifer and everyone else will like it too."

"They'll be surprised," I say.

Mom laughs. "They will definitely be surprised."

When I get to the kitchen, Dad is already there. He's in his robe and slippers. The three of us work together to get everything ready. We set the table, hang decorations, cut fruit, and put everything in bowls and on platters.

"Time to go," says Dad when we're done.

I look at the clock. It's 7 a.m. We're right on schedule.

"Mallory, you ride with Mom in the van,"
says Dad. "I'll follow in my car."

All of a sudden, I feel nervous. "Mom,
what if this doesn't make up for what
happened?"

Mom stops and looks at me. "Mallory, you made a mistake. People make mistakes. What you're doing is very sweet. I think Chloe Jennifer and your friends will see that you want to do the right thing." She smiles at me. "I have a feeling everything will work out fine."

I hope Mom is right. There's only one way to find out. I grab the list I made last night. It has the addresses of all the girls in my class on it. I follow Mom and Dad outside.

It's time to put my plan into action.

Our first stop is at Zoe's house. When we pull up, Mom winks at me. "Go on in," she says. "Zoe's mom is expecting you."

It feels funny to be knocking on someone's door so early, but when I do, Zoe's mom opens it right away and leads the way to Zoe's room.

When I get there, I shake Zoe's shoulder. "Wake up!" I say. When she opens her eyes, she looks confused to see me there.

"I'm having a surprise birthday breakfast for Chloe Jennifer," I explain. "It's like a party before the party. My mom and dad are outside in their cars, and we're going to pick up all the girls in our class and bring them to my house for breakfast. You're the first one, and Chloe Jennifer will be the last. That way, everyone will be there to wake up the birthday girl."

Zoe blinks like she's still half-asleep and not really following what I'm saying. "I have to get dressed," she says.

"You're already dressed!" I tell her. "It's a *come-as-you-are* party. You can wear your pj's."

Zoe grins like this part of the plan sounds good to her. "Then what are we waiting for?"

She slips her feet into her slippers and follows me to the van.

From there we pick up Brittany, April, Dawn, Pamela, Arielle, Danielle, Emma, and Grace.

"We just have to make two more stops," I say once Mom's van is full.

I don't say it out loud to my friends, but I'm nervous about the last two stops.

When we pull up in front of Mary Ann's house, I cross my toes inside my fuzzy duck slippers. I really hope this works.

I knock, and Colleen opens the door. I head straight to Mary Ann's room. "Wake up," I whisper to her. I have to whisper it a bunch of times before it works.

Mary Ann opens her eyes a little, and then she opens them really wide, like she doesn't know what I'm doing in her room and isn't sure she likes seeing me here.

Since Mary Ann still isn't talking to me, I start explaining right away.

I tell Mary Ann about my party-before-the-party plan. "I wanted to do something extra-extra-extra nice for Chloe Jennifer," I say. When I'm done explaining, I recross my toes inside my fuzzy duck slippers. I hope hearing about the party-before-the-party will finally make Mary Ann un-mad at me—at least un-mad enough to go along with my plan.

When I'm done talking, Mary Ann is quiet. I'm not sure if it's because she just woke up or because she doesn't know what to say.

I look at her like I really mean what I'm about to say next. "I felt terrible about everything that happened."

"I feel terrible too," says Mary Ann. She pauses. Then she adds, "Mallory, we need to talk."

I nod and then give Mary Ann a *we'll-have-to-talk-later-because-right-now-we've-got-a-surprise-breakfast-party-to-get-to* look.

Mary Ann smiles like she understands everything I'm not saying in a way only a best friend could. I let out a deep breath.

I know that smile is Mary Ann's way of saying that we're still best friends and always will be.

I look at the clock by Mary Ann's bed. It's almost 8 a.m. "C'mon!" I grab Mary Ann's arm. "We have to get to Chloe Jennifer's before she wakes up!"

Mary Ann slips her feet into her slippers, and we race out of her house. The other girls pile out of Mom's van and Dad's car. We all run across the street to Chloe Jennifer's house. When we get there, Chloe Jennifer's mom opens the door before we even knock. She has a big smile on her face. "I was expecting you girls," she says softly.

We all try not to giggle as we tiptoe back to Chloe Jennifer's room. When we get there, I push open the door. We all rush in and jump onto her bed.

"SURPRISE!" we all yell.

Chloe Jennifer's eyes fly open. She looks as shocked as if someone just dumped a bucket of ice water on her.

"HAPPY BIRTHDAY!" we shout.

After I explain that I planned a surprise party-before-her-party, I pause. I have something else to tell her that's more

important. It's also a lot harder to say.

I clear my throat and begin. "Chloe Jennifer, I'm really sorry I cut off your pigtail. It was a terrible thing to do. And I'm sorry I haven't been very nice to you since you moved here. I really hope you'll forgive me, and I hope you have a super-happy birthday."

Chloe Jennifer grins. "It's OK," she says. Then she hops out of bed and gives me a big hug. "Thanks, Mallory. It's really sweet of you to help make my birthday so special." She slips her feet into her slippers. "Let's get the party started!"

When we get to my house, Chloe Jennifer is even more surprised to see all the food and decorations. "It's a *Do-It-Yourself* birthday breakfast," I tell my friends.

They crowd around the table. It's covered with bowls and platters piled high with tons of breakfast goodies. "You can put whatever you want on your plate and make your own breakfast," I explain. "The crazier, the better!"

My friends start filling up plates with pancakes and waffles and decorating them with the toppings we put out—maple syrup and whipped cream and all kinds of fruit.

"Look at this," says April. She shows us a pancake that she decorated to look like a flower.

Pamela makes her bagel into a clown.

Arielle and Danielle make their waffles look like patchwork quilts.

When everyone is done making plates, we all crowd into the living room. "Who's ready to watch *Fashion Fran*?" I ask.

Everyone cheers. All my friends like *Fashion Fran*.

I turn on the TV and head for the couch, but someone grabs my arm before I can sit down. That someone is Mary Ann. "Mallory, can I talk to you?" she asks.

I nod and follow her to my room.

She makes me sit down on my bed, and then she starts talking.

"Mallory, I've been mad at you because I didn't understand why you weren't being nice to Chloe Jennifer. I didn't get why you wouldn't like her, so I just kept trying extra hard to include her." Mary Ann pauses. "But I did a lot of things wrong too."

Mary Ann picks at a loose thread on my bedspread.

"I know I made too big of a deal about the whole look-alike thing."

Mary Ann keeps picking at my bedspread while she talks. "Chloe Jennifer talked to me about it yesterday. She said that even though we look alike, she doesn't want to make a big deal about it. She told me that it makes her feel uncomfortable. She said that even though we're a lot alike, we don't have to be exactly the same."

Mary Ann pauses, but she's not done. After a second, she adds, "She could tell that you felt left out when I wanted to be twins with her for the dance. She said it has probably been hard for you to get used to her being here, and us being look-alikes made it worse. I hadn't thought about it that way before."

"I tried to tell you how I was feeling," I say.

"I know," she says. "I should've listened." She's quiet for a minute like she's having a hard time finding the right words.

When she starts talking again, her voice is soft. "And I shouldn't have told you our friendship was over," she says. "We've been best friends all our lives. Having Chloe Jennifer around doesn't mean we can't still be best friends with each other. It just means we can have another good friend too."

I nod. "I get that now," I say. "I was just worried that you liked Chloe Jennifer more than you liked me."

Mary Ann takes a deep breath. "Mallory, I'm sorry I said I didn't want to be best friends anymore. You will always be my best friend."

Wow! I never thought Mary Ann would be saying she was sorry.

And I *really* can't believe Chloe Jennifer was the one who understood how I was feeling and explained it to Mary Ann. That was really sweet of Chloe Jennifer.

"Thanks for understanding," I tell Mary Ann.

Mary Ann holds up her pinky. "Best friends forever," she says.

"Forever," I say. I hook my pinky around hers. We shake pinkies, and then we hug.

We're still hugging when I hear a knock on my door. Chloe Jennifer opens it. "May I come in?" she asks softly.

Mary Ann and I both nod. I scoot over to make room for her on the bed.

"Mallory, thanks for the party," she says after she sits down. "It was really sweet of you to do that for me."

She pauses, and then she says, "When I first got here, I was so sad about leaving Atlanta. I had a best friend there who'd been my best friend my whole life—kind of like you and Mary Ann. I didn't want to leave her and didn't know if I would make new friends in Fern Falls."

I think back to when Chloe Jennifer said she was scared to go to a new school. All I could think about then was how I didn't want Mary Ann and Chloe Jennifer to become best friends. I didn't pay attention to how she was feeling.

"Moving is hard," I say to Chloe Jennifer.
She smiles like she knows I get it.

"Mallory, I know you and Mary Ann are
best friends," says Chloe Jennifer. "I never
want to ruin that. I just hope I can be
friends with both of you."

Maybe it's because she's an only child
and has spent a lot of time around adults,
but what Chloe Jennifer is saying seems
really mature to me. I want to say just the
right thing back.

I think about the day Chloe Jennifer
moved to Wish Pond Road. A lot has
happened since then. Some bad things. But
some good things too.

I found something new I like to eat at
the mall.

I got my best grade ever on a science
project.

And best of all, I've made a nice new friend.

"Of course you can be our friend," I tell Chloe Jennifer. "I think the three of us can have a lot of fun together."

She smiles like that's the best birthday present she could get today.

And the best part is . . . I like giving it.

A SURPRISE!

It's been a long day. Chloe Jennifer has already had two parties. But the day isn't over yet. There's another surprise that's about to happen on Wish Pond Road, and it's the best one of the day.

I walk next door to Mary Ann's house and ring the bell.

"It's time," I say when she answers. She hooks her arm through mine, and we walk across the street to Chloe Jennifer's house.

Her parents told me we should come over at 4, and it's 3:58.

"Remember, act like you don't know anything," I say to Mary Ann as we cross the street.

She presses her finger and thumb together and runs them across her mouth like she's zipping her lips shut.

When we knock on the door, Chloe Jennifer answers. She looks surprised to see us.

I say exactly what her mom told me to say. "We wanted to see all your birthday presents."

Chloe Jennifer smiles. "C'mon in." We follow her into the kitchen, where her birthday presents are piled on the table. We start oohing and aahing as she shows us everything she got.

"Would you girls like another piece of cake?" Chloe Jennifer's mom asks.

Mary Ann and I both nod, but I'm so excited that I don't know how I'll be able to eat cake. Just as Chloe Jennifer's mom finishes cutting our slices, we hear a car honk in the driveway.

"Your dad is home with the groceries," Chloe Jennifer's mom says. Then she looks at Mary Ann and me. "Would you girls mind helping us carry some bags inside?"

As we get up to follow Chloe Jennifer outside, her mom winks at Mary Ann and me.

It's finally time! I can't wait to see the look on Chloe Jennifer's face when she finds out what Mary Ann and I already know.

As we walk outside, Chloe Jennifer's dad is coming up the sidewalk, but he isn't carrying grocery bags. He has a small crate. He puts the crate down in front of Chloe Jennifer, opens it, and takes out a little brown-and-white-spotted puppy.

He carefully hands the puppy to Chloe Jennifer. "Special delivery for the birthday girl," he says.

"Surprise!" Chloe Jennifer's parents and Mary Ann and I all say at the same time.

Chloe Jennifer looks confused, like she's not sure this is really happening. "He's mine?" she asks her dad.

He nods. "Mom and I told you we were waiting for the right time to get a dog. We think turning ten is a pretty good time."

We all watch as Chloe Jennifer hugs the puppy to her chest. "Mom, Dad, thank you so much! Thank you! Thank you! Thank you!" she says. Then she looks at me like she wants to be sure it's OK that she said it three times.

I grin. "Three people saying things three times is better than two."

Chloe Jennifer smiles. Then sits down on

the porch swing with the puppy on her lap. Her mom starts taking pictures.

"Mom, take a picture of all of us," says Chloe Jennifer.

Mary Ann and I sit down on either side of her. Her mom takes a picture. Chloe Jennifer puts the puppy right up to her face and kisses his nose. "I'm going to call you Freckles," she says, looking into the puppy's spotted face.

I grin and reach over to pet Freckles. "That's a perfect name."

"We'll leave you girls and Freckles alone for a while," says Chloe Jennifer's dad.

As they start to walk inside, they're smiling at each other like they're happy they finally gave in and got Chloe Jennifer the present she wanted most.

And they're not the only ones who are happy. I'm happy too. Chloe Jennifer is a

really sweet friend. I'm glad she's had such a good birthday.

I push the swing a little with my foot. We start to move back and forth.

Freckles lets out a little sigh, like all the swinging is making him sleepy.

I think back to how I felt when Chloe Jennifer moved here. I was so sure that she and Mary Ann and I could never all be friends. I thought three was a crowd. But now that I've gotten to know her, I know that's not true.

Mary Ann and I might have our differences. We might even argue sometimes. But I know she'll always be my best friend.

And now we have a new friend. A friend I like a lot.

Mary Ann and Chloe Jennifer and I all push the swing with our feet. As we lift higher in the air, nobody says a word. It's weird, but it's like we all know that no one has to say anything.

Just the three of us sitting together on the swing is enough.

POETICALLY SPEAKING

I don't know if you ever write poetry, but after everything that happened with Chloe Jennifer, I felt inspired to make up a poem for her.

The truth is that since her birthday, Chloe Jennifer and Mary Ann and I have been having a lot of fun together. I, Mallory McDonald, never thought I would be saying this, but three really can be good company.

Chloe Jennifer really liked the poem I wrote, and I hope you do too!

Three's Company!

By Mallory McDonald

The best things in life come in
groups of three.

The first letters of the alphabet:
A, B, and C.

The very first numbers: one, two,
and three.

Three little piggies, as cute as can be!

Three blind mice (even though they
can't see!)

Three kittens without mittens
(go on a shopping spree!)

Three bears chased Goldilocks
up a tree!

Three Musketeers. Best candy ever.
Trust me!!

Vanilla, chocolate, and strawberry.
Best ice cream combo, I guarantee!

Three great friends: You, Mary Ann,
and me!

I'm glad you moved to Wish Pond Road!
It fills my heart with glee!

I have one thing to say: Whoopee!
Whoopee! Whoopee!

Big, huge hugs and kisses!!
Mallory

DIY BREAKFAST

One more thing: If you decide to have a surprise wake-up party (which would be a great decision because surprise wake-up parties are fun, fun, fun!), you should definitely have a Do-It-Yourself Breakfast. My friends loved it, and I think yours will too.

Here's the recipe.

Have fun doing it yourself!

DIY BREAKFAST (Serves 10–12)

Ingredients:

2 boxes mini pancakes
2 boxes mini waffles
2 boxes French toast sticks
1 bag of mini bagels
1 jar of peanut butter
1 jar of strawberry jelly
1 tub of cream cheese
strawberries, banana slices, and grapes
   in separate bowls
chocolate chips and marshmallows in
   separate bowls
powdered sugar in a shaker
cinnamon sugar in a shaker
maple syrup
butter or margarine

You will also need:
a tablecloth, paper plates, napkins, plastic
knives and forks, and frilly toothpicks

Directions:

Set up a table with a pretty paper tablecloth (I like pink and purple, but any color will work). You can decorate the table (which I did) with flowers, confetti, or better yet, both!

Put out paper plates, napkins, plastic knives, and frilly toothpicks. Arrange all the ingredients in the center of the table so your friends can get to everything easily.

You will need to ask your parents to help you cook the pancakes and waffles and French toast sticks.

When the smell of fresh breakfast fills the air, invite your friends over to the table and let them make their own breakfast creations. Don't forget to take pictures before everyone eats it all up.

Variations:

You can change up the ingredients. Just pick things you think your friends would like. Pineapple, kiwi, coconut, chocolate sauce, meatballs... (Ew! Just kidding! But if you think your friends would like meatballs on their pancakes, go ahead and try it!)

Yum! Yum! Yum!

Have fun, fun, fun!

Darby Creek
A division of Lerner Publishing Group, Inc.
241 First Avenue North
Minneapolis, MN 55401 USA

For reading levels and more information, look up this title at
www.lernerbooks.com

Cover background: © Zigi/Bigstock.com.

Main body text set in LuMarcLL 14/20. Typeface provided by Linotype.

Library of Congress Cataloging-in-Publication Data

Friedman, Laurie B., 1964—
    Three's company, Mallory! / by Laurie Friedman ; illustrations by Jennifer
Kalis.
        p.   cm. — (Mallory ; #21)
    Summary: When Chloe Jennifer moves to Wish Pond Road, Mallory's friend
Mary Ann starts including Chloe Jennifer in everything that she and Mallory
do—but in Mallory's opinion, three is a crowd.
    ISBN 978-1-4677-0921-7 (trade hard cover : alk. paper)
    ISBN 978-1-4677-2413-5 (eBook)
    [1. Best friends—Fiction. 2. Friendship—Fiction. 3. Jealousy—Fiction.]
I. Kalis, Jennifer, illustrator. II. Title. III. Title: Three is company, Mallory
PZ7.F89773Thr 2014
[Fic]—dc23   2013018613

Manufactured in the United States of America
2 — BP — 12/15/14